For Mike, Katy and Kit - with all my love
J.B.
For Gillian
S. M.

First published in 2013 by Nosy Crow Ltd
The Crow's Nest, 10a Lant Street
London SE1 1QR
www.nosycrow.com

ISBN 978 0 85763 089 6 (HB)
ISBN 978 0 85763 090 2 (PB)

Nosy Crow and associated logos are trademarks and /or registered trademarks
of Nosy Crow Ltd.

A CIP catalogue record for this book is available
from the British Library.

Printed in China

1 3 5 7 9 8 6 4 2 (HB)
1 3 5 7 9 8 6 4 2 (PB)

Books

Always Everywhere

Jane Blatt

Illustrated by

Sarah Massini

nosy crow

Book big

elephant

Book small

Book wide

Mummy and Me

Book tall

Book build

Book mat

Book
chair

Book
hat

Book
park

Book
shop

Book start

Book stop

Book
scary

Book
funny

PEEK-A-BOO
A peephole book
to make you giggle
and chortle and chuckle
and roar with laughter.

100
JUNGLE
JOKES

SILLY
BILLY

banana

Book rainy

In sunshine
or in rain,
every day is
a story day.

Happy Days

Book sunny

Book give

Book share

Books always . . .

. . . . every

where.